This edition published by Parragon Books Ltd in 2015 and distributed by

Parragon Inc.
440 Park Avenue South, 13th Floor
New York, NY 10016
www.parragon.com

ISBN 978-1-4748-3515-2

Printed in China

One More Rabbit ...

PaRragon

Bath • New York • Cologne • Melbourne • Delhi
Hong Kong • Shenzhen • Singapore • Amsterdam

Once upon a time, in a hollow tree stump,
lived **ONE** excited rabbit with ...

one
loving mother and ...

one
loving father and ...

two

helpful sisters and ...

three

not-so-helpful brothers and ...

four
music-loving
uncles and ...

five
busy aunts and ...

six
troublemaking
cousins and ...

seven

impatient second cousins and ...

eight

merry third cousins and ...

two
grooving grandmothers and ...

two

grooving grandfathers and ...

four talented great grandmothers and ...

four talented great grandfathers and ...

eight
toe-tapping great great
grandmothers and ...

eight

toe-tapping great great
grandfathers and ...

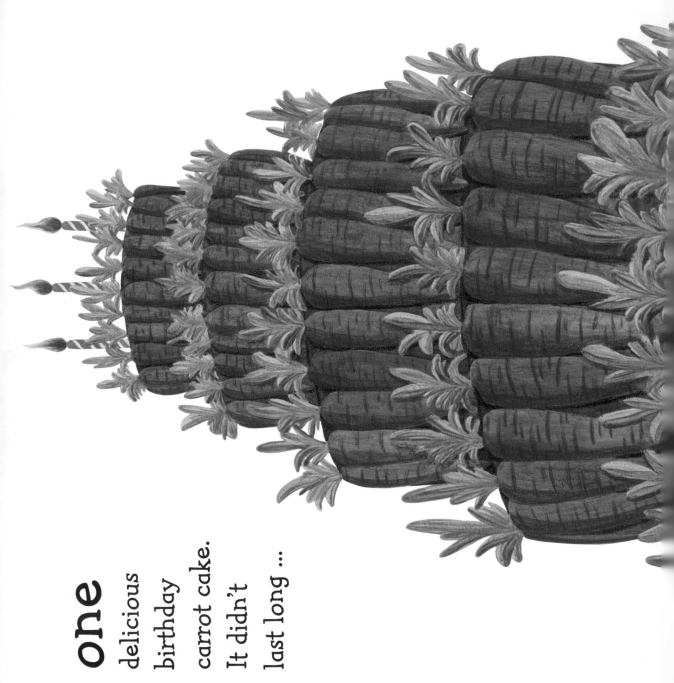

one
delicious
birthday
carrot cake.
It didn't
last long …

They were a **BIG,** warm rabbit family,
all in **one** clump.

And they **all** celebrated together
in a hollow tree stump ...

with a little excited rabbit
who was learning how to jump!